William Forsyth

A Lay of Lochleven

William Forsyth

A Lay of Lochleven

ISBN/EAN: 9783337427337

Printed in Europe, USA, Canada, Australia, Japan

Cover: Foto ©Andreas Hilbeck / pixelio.de

More available books at **www.hansebooks.com**

A LAY

OF

LOCHLEVEN.

BY

WILLIAM O' YE WEST.

"MUCH ADO ABOUT NOTHING."

GLASGOW:

ROBERT FORRESTER, 1 ROYAL EXCHANGE SQUARE.

1887.

GLASGOW:

PRINTED BY ROBERT ANDERSON, 22 ANN STREET.

DEDICATED

TO THE

MEMBERS OF THE ST. MUNGO ANGLING CLUB,

GLASGOW,

IN APPRECIATION OF THEIR

MERITS AS ANGLERS AND THEIR WORTH AS MEN.

PREFATORY NOTE.

N explanatory note is due to any reader outside the circle to which this production is dedicated, and at whose instigation it is published, who may honour it with a perusal.

At the close of the fishing season, two years ago, the council of the Saint Mungo Angling Club, Glasgow, actuated by a desire to enjoy a rehearsal of the tough and tugging runs of that and previous years, arranged to hold during the winter season monthly meetings of the Club; and, to promote fraternal intercourse amongst the members, it was resolved to meet on the first Tuesday in each month.

As was anticipated, these meetings turned out to be both enjoyable and instructive. From the first they assumed a literary and critical character. Many papers of an exceedingly interesting and edifying import were read, on which each member was invited by our esteemed president, "Uranus," to offer his opinion.

While many papers very appropriately bore largely on the How, Where, When, and with What to fish, they were not necessarily restricted to the technicalities of the gentle art. The discussion of localities, tackle, the various kinds of lures and methods of fishing, frequently formed staple articles of supply; while imaginary, humorous, and descriptive papers were freely admitted : hence the appearance of the "Lay"—an original conception of an absolutely impossible occurrence metrically expressed.

Perhaps no body of men repairing to fish the prolific casts of Lochleven could be selected better able to bear the brunt of the imaginary blank chronicled in the "Lay" than the Members of St. Mungo. This Club includes in its membership some skilful, well-known veteran anglers—anglers who have for years footed the heather together, wandered amidst the quiet beauty of our haughs and glens, and by many a mossy-margined stream,

> Wi' lairs whare fish can jouk and hide
> Awa frae human ken ;

and who, above most men, can in a very special sense realise and appreciate the full import of the utterance—

> "We twa hae paidl't i' the burn
> Frae morning sun till dine."

In addition to the epauletted old warriors, there are many others whose zeal and enthusiasm in the gentle art cannot fail to equip them as worthy followers of their seniors in maintaining the prestige of the Club and the reputation which some of these old warriors have so deservedly earned.

The St. Mungo compares favourably with any other club visiting this loch. In 1884 it ranked as the Premier Club of Scotland, having in an equal number of competitions captured a greater number and creeled a heavier weight of trout than any other club during that year, or for fourteen years prior to that date; while the "Jeems" of the "Lay" carried off the championship of Lochleven. These are achievements of which any club may justly be proud.

The "Lay" was a somewhat hurried production. It is not issued as a specimen of the quality of the papers read, but as a trifling conceit written to fill up the time of a meeting at which a very graphic and amusing paper was read by one of the most genial and gifted sons of St. Mungo. The writer was much surprised, if not flattered by its reception by the Club, who unanimously voted its immediate publication.

With much reserve, and a depressing sense of its manifold imperfections, he now complies with that request. Haunted by a dread of adverse criticism, he fears that in his rashness he has failed to act upon the wisdom of the old proverb that

"A man wi' riven breeks should sit still."

Whatever may be the fate of the "Lay," it has already been stamped with the approval and authority of the Club: it is published under its auspices. The writer clings to the hope that it may escape the "east wind" of withering comment — a wind which, with rare exceptions, chills the ardour, blights the sport, and quenches the hope of the angler—hope, the most lasting emotion which lingers in his heart.

By some the illustrations may be characterised as crude. Perhaps they are; and that an apology may be required for their appearance. It is permissible to state, however, that they are the productions of a novice, who, like the writer of the "Lay," makes no pretence to authorship in the line herein essayed.

It is hoped, however, that the portraits will not fail to lend a little attraction to the Lay, even at the risk of unkennelling the anonymity so jealously sought to be preserved. The reasons for this reticence about names will be as apparent to the outside reader as they are to the members of the "inner circle." Few men, and certainly few anglers, would care to confront such characterizations and maledictions, even although the imprecator was only a "portly fish."

The "Lay" is intended to point a moral, and the moral is uniformly applicable to angling, wherever and under whatever form it is followed:—

> When balmy Spring your hopes high pitch,
> And thrills your souls with angling itch,
> All you who this true legend read
> Of your intent let none take heed ;
> With soft and stealthy step draw near—
> Beware of trouts 'neath tree and pier.

GLASGOW, *May, 1887.*

"The old grey keep, the castle hoar,
Still seen from Leven's sedgy shore."

See page 11.

A LAY OF LOCHLEVEN.

LOCHLEVEN'S old historic tide,

Which erst had sheltered Scotland's pride

When strife and turmoil shook the throne,

Retreat was found in island lone.

The old grey keep, the castle hoar,

Still seen from Leven's sedgy shore,

Draws pilgrims from each foreign clime

To gaze on that which, in its prime,

Imprisoned Scotland's hapless Queen,

Unrobed and reft of royal sheen.

What thoughts were hers! Ah! who can tell

What tumults wild her bosom swell!

What wild'ring fears and doubts arise

To wound her heart, to cloud her eyes:

From palace driven to lonesome keep,

To pine alone in anguish deep;

Imprisoned, captive, held in thrall ;

No longer courted, loved by all :

An outcast caged on lonely isle ;

Nought left to soothe or to beguile

The tedium of her hapless fate ;

To shield her 'gainst a faction's hate.

Dark were her thoughts, her prospects drear ;

No ray of hope to gild or cheer ;

No longer peers and courtiers bow,

Or gallant yeomen take the vow;

Torn from the pomp she prized erewhile—

Reft of her crown, all regal style;

Denied the homage of a smile.

With blighted hopes and broken crest,

Doomed with the mean to herd and rest;

Withdrawn the warrior's proffered aid—

His life, his honour, and his blade;

No Minstrel's tale salutes her ear—

Silenced the harp she loved so dear;

No courtiers fain her presence throng

To fling the jest or raise the song.

Ah! brilliant scenes, so joyous, gay;

To irksome solitude give way:

Pent and immured in hated keep,

Nought left but o'er the past to weep;

While base-born kerns keep watch and ward

O'er captive, held close under guard.

(How fitful fortune's changeful sway,

By fickle freaks in one brief day

Steals from our grasp the joys we prize,

Wounds the sad heart and blinds the eyes.)

At dusk, ere day had closed its eye,

She sought retreat in turret high—

Retreat from menials' prying gaze—

To muse on bright, on better days.

The Leven's placid western flow,

'Neath setting sun's soft amber glow,

Restful and calm, assuaged her woe.

Pensive and sad, she seized the lyre,

This plaint of mingled grief and ire

Poured slowly forth, through blinding tears,

And told, as caught by listening ears,
To men through long-descending years:—

Mary's Wail.

In this dark hour of anguish 'tis bootless to wail;
To burden the breeze with my grief-laden tale;
To waft to the home where my young days were spent
The dark tale of sorrow my bosom hath rent:

Ah! dear, happy days, ye can never return;
There's nought left me now but to weep and to mourn;
To pine o'er the past, o'er friends scattered and gone:
My sad heart is hopeless, now blighted and lone.

Oh, fain would I flee like a bird o'er the main,
Far, far from all pomp, that I freedom might gain—
Revisit the dear friends of life's early day,
When my bosom was ardent; life, joyous and gay.

No more will I join in bright courtly array,
To smile on the gallants who bent to my sway:
Ah! how fitful and fleeting those scenes of my pride;
All fled, like the traitors who lurked by my side.

Deserted, and reft of my kingdom and crown,
My sceptre is shattered, despoiled my renown;
Held captive; no leal heart, no kinsman to shield ;
Dire fate now confronts me, to which I must yield.

Like the mist of the morn slow melting away,
Or the foliage of summer 'neath autumn's decay,
My friends and my fortune: my life's overcast
Like a sore beaten bark in a drear winter blast.

But why thus repine o'er a guilt-laden past?
Why deplore earthly joys, too sordid to last—
Illusive and fleeting, oft fraught with a sting?
I'd fain rise to Heaven, tho' on faltering wing.

My heart's worn and weary; I've wantonly strayed ;
In my weakness I've erred; was through passion betrayed:
God knows how I wandered : how wicked, how vile !
O'er a drear-wasted past all my thoughts me revile.

I'm bent 'neath the load of my folly and shame ;
My soul was too ardent; consumed by its flame,
Allured by the wiles of the flatterer's tongue
I surrendered my honour, while taintless and young.

To love too confiding—too wayward and free,

I yielded and fell. Ah! how could I foresee

That an impulse so tender, a passion so pure,

Could e'er from my heart all its happiness lure.

Remorse for my weakness o'erwhelms my dark soul;

My fears, my disquiet I cannot control:

Ah! *Ave Maria*, I clemency crave ;

An outcast and helpless—thou only can'st save:

I'm in darkness and doubt, in swelt'ring amaze;

Oh! send forth thy light through a rift in the haze ;

Dispel my deep gloom, o'ershadow my path ;

Me rescue and shelter from vengeance and wrath:

Life's pride and its passions, Oh! cleanse thou away;

I fear not the future if thou art my stay:

Oh! dry the tears shed o'er a vain, erring life,

And, peaceful and pure, let me yield up its strife:

On thee I rely, to thee trustingly cling;

A soiled, penitent heart is all I can bring:

Oh! spurn not the prayer of a soul tempest-tost;

Unless thou enclasp me, I'm ruined, I'm lost.

Thus pined this captive of the keep,

Nor found repose in soothing sleep;

Long nights she lists the hooting owl

And moaning wind through turrets howl;

The eerie creaking of the trees

'Neath lonely sough of quickened breeze:

With crowding thoughts, heart sad and lone

Mourns days and scenes now lost and gone.

From restless couch, with feverish brain

The weary eye oft seeks the main;

Pants for the liberty of yore:

To hoist her standard on the shore,

To vanquish traitors, quell their hate,

Retrieve her throne, reshape her fate;

Her honour gain, assert her cause,

And to her country give its laws.

Oft at the dawn of morning's light,

The freedom of the swallow's flight

Careering through the ambient air

O'er Leven's bosom broad and fair;

Oft, ere the noon had touched its height,

The graceful sea-gull's circling flight,

Or floating free on crested wave

Which round her prison home did lave;

Or oft at close of waning day

Each bird lilts blithe on chosen spray;

The sun, slow sinking in the west,—

On these she mused, sad and opprest.

Sights such as these, dark shadows fling;

Her heart and soul with anguish wring,

Recalling days when light and free

As milk-maid tripping o'er the lea;

Light as the linnet on the thorn,

Blithe as the lark at flush of morn—

Days when, 'mid throngs in Holyrood,

In matchless beauty forth she stood:

In grace and mien transcending all

In camp, or court, or festive hall.

Now all is changed! her sceptre's gone;

Betrayed, deserted, banished, lone.

O'er cherished friends, o'er early years,

'Tis bootless shedding bitter tears,

For tears are now of no avail;

Her captive chains all hopes impale:

Disloyal hordes in numbers grow—

No dauntless heart to strike a blow

To rescue and restore her throne ;

Her barons false, her troopers flown ;

Her dastard chiefs outrage her laws,

Leave laggards to maintain her cause.

Through Douglas—brave historic name,

Name known on many a field of fame—

Ere many moons had waxed and waned,

By well-laid schemes her freedom gained:

Disguised, she fled, she reached the shore,

Her dreary keep to see no more.

In the long galaxy of fame

There stands no more conspicuous name—

Name better known in the long roll

Inscribed on our illustrious scroll.

A gentle nature, beauteous form,

Ill fitted to withstand a storm ;

A haughty spirit, ardent, keen

Of courage, as became a Queen !

Inconstant, fickle in her aims ;

Exacting, violent in her claims;

Oft erring in her choice of friends;

Unscrupulous to attain her ends;

Beset, betrayed by treach'rous art;

Impelled to play unworthy part,

Which tarnished, sullied her fair fame,

Nor lent a halo to her name;

Romantic, young, advent'rous, bold—

Tale more pathetic ne'er was told!

Away hath passed these elder days,

So oft the theme of Minstrel's lays;

No clash of arms, no courtly strife,

Now thrills the Minstrel's harp with life;

Sweet Peace now crowns the sparkling tide

Of Leven's swell, the Angler's pride;

Yet doughty deeds and feats of skill

Still rouse the Muse—with heart and will

To tell of quest through drift and bay,—

Of such I sing, come! list the lay:

'Twas on a sultry eve in June,

O'er eastern heights the full-orbed moon

Rose calm and clear with silvery ray,

As if to greet the waning day;

See page 23.

" Near Black, their Commodore, they stood,
While he thus spoke in counselling mood " —

Lochleven gleamed with amber bright,

'Neath halo caught from western light;

The breeze was still, the tide at rest,

The fleet-winged swallow skimmed its breast,

The wild duck sought its reedy lair,

And myriad insects filled the air.

Each oar was hushed, each boat lay near,

The boatmen gathered at the pier:

Near Black, their Commodore, they stood,

While thus he spoke in counselling mood—

" Keep clear heads for to-morrow's fray,

St. Mungo has bespoke the day;

More eager men, of keener zest,

Ne'er searched Lochleven's ample breast.

Each bank and bay, each stretch and strand,

Where'er ye think a trout ye'll land,

Fish freely with selecting care—

Of empty creels, 'clean' boats, beware!

The Club will vie with all the West,

To garland green anew its crest."

Meantime, while Black addressed his crew,

Beneath the pier, concealed from view,

A portly fish, of ample size,

Of girth and length which anglers prize,

With upturned eye and list'ning ear,

Heard cruel schemes planned on the pier;

To try by every art and wile

Of fly and phantom, to beguile,

To lure, to kill, and shed the blood

Of harmless tenants of the flood.

Fears for his kinsmen wrung his heart.

Thoughtful and sad he sought the " Scart,"

Fleet scouts sent out, through deep and bay,

To warn them of the coming day.

Ere morning dawn, a countless host

Had gathered from each teeming coast,

And crowding thronged intent to hear

The doleful tidings of the pier.

With aspect sad, in gravest mood

Up spoke this monarch of the flood :

These warning counsels forth he flung

To list'ning shoals which round him clung :—

The Trout's Address.

" Kindred and freends, len' me your ear ;

Come! gather roun'; tae me draw near,

While I impart tae kinsmen dear

    A warnin' word,

Which a' should fill wi' cautious fear,

    In deep and ford.

" Yestreen, while saunt'rin' tae the west,

The sun was low, the Loch at rest ;

Unseen, close 'neath the pier I prest,

    And heard, wi' dreid,

Blude-thirsty schemes which wrung ma breast,

    By men o'erheid :

" Black, first tae speak ; I heard him say—

' To-morrow is St. Mungo's Day :

Mair skilly loons ne'er sought the fray,

    Tae catch and kill ;

Prepare tae search ilk drift and bay,

    Their creels tae fill.

" ' Let ilk man here be on his mettle ;

Wi' clear heids, come in best o' fettle ;

Wi' hand on oar, let ilk man ettle
Tae dae his best:
St. Mungo's men the rest will settle,
And guard their crest.'

" Black's greedy ee scanned east and wast ;
The sinkin' sun was noo o'ercast ;
He said, ' Nae signs o' comin' blast ;
Ye're day's work's done,
If balmy warmth till mornin' last ;
Ye'll get rare fun !'

" The hungry hoond expressed the hope
St. Mungo's wadna fail tae cope
Wi' ony club o' equal scope,
Tae bear the gree :
Had I the maigs tae use a rope,
He'd dree his dree :

" I'd strap him tae a sunken tree,
Tae writhe and wriggle till he'd dee ;
Watch greedy pike tear oot his ee ;
Lie till he'd rot :
And maggots breed we'd ee wi' glee
In pool or pot.

" BLACK."

See page 23

" URANUS."

See page 31.

" Oh, wad some kelpie seize that sweep !

And droon him in mid water, deep,

Whare slimy eels wad through him creep,

His entrails gnaw :

Nae inmate o' the Loch wad weep

O'er his closed maw.

" For years, this cruel, cunnin' squief

Has filled oor hearts wi' dool and grief ;

Tae see him deid wad bring relief :

We'd plaudits raise—

Cheers led by me, your ancient chief,

In Kelpie's praise.

" To-day, the Club will try its skill,

Intent and keen oor blude tae spill,

And he wha maist o' us can kill,

Will gain the prize.

Come, list ! this is ma royal will—

Avoid their flees.

" Uranus, leader o' the van

O' Mungo's mean and murd'rous clan ;

Concocting aye some heartless plan,

    Oor kind tae kill ;

Has aften stood as foremost man,

    Through ruthless skill.

" Loch Lomond's ' Black Nebs ' he may seize

Wi' coarser cast, and bigger flees ;

Let him their greedy thrapples squeeze,

    'Tis their look-oot ;

Oor kindred here's mair ill tae please :

    The wale o' troot.

" O' his slim gossamer beware ;

His tackle's fine, his hooks are spare ;

He plies his craft wi' greedy care—

    Keep aff his boat ;

His treach'rous flees owre aft ensnare—

    Sae licht they float.

" Douce Dot, their ' Scribe,' he's quite as bad ;

A pawky, eager, dang'rous lad ;

His feats o' skill aft drive me mad

    Wi' passion, tost—

Mak' me, and countless neibors, sad,

    For kindred lost.

"DOUCE DOT."

See page 32.

C

"ANDREW."

See page 37.

" Tak tent ! his quiet cunnin' shun ;

If ye wad leeve tae hae mair fun,

And up oor streams in wedlock run,

Gie Dot the slip ;

Send him ashore ' clean,' baffled, done—

Bitin' his lip.

" Andrew and Jeems, that blatant pair !

Whase noise micht aft the hale Loch scare ;

Yet, o' their well-plied rods beware,

They're men o' skill ;

They'll raither heize ye'r heids through air,

Than fail tae kill :

" They'll prowl and plot and scheme, a' day,

Roun' ilka headlan', bank, and bay ;

Try meanest wiles oor kind tae slay,

Tae crood their creel :

Raither than they should on me prey,

I'd face the Deil.

" Andrew, their ' Vice,' aft wrings ma heart;

Tears kith and kin sae aft apart ;

His temptin' flees and cruel art
  Work fell despair:
Send him adrift, tae delve and scart
   His ' Lands near Ayr.'

" Brusk Jeems the keen, aye on the watch,
 Tries foulest means oor kind tae catch;
 Oor back or belly he will snatch;
   E'en snap his cast,
Sae fain tae rank first in the scratch—
   His purpose blast.

" Lithe Teviotdale's amang the worst;
 And, as oor foe, I rank him first:
 Aft in oor blude he slakes his thirst,
   Ere early morn;
Tae me his very trade's accurst,
   Fills me wi' scorn.

" I hate his craft! that artfu' Deil
 Can busk a hook or build a creel;
 Supply his mates wi' rod and reel;
   Gie coonsels mean:
If tae ma will ye wad prove leal—
   Send him hame clean.

"JEEMS."

See page 37.

"LITHE TEVIOTDALE."

See page 38.

" Tweedie and Jeff, men free o' strife,

    May, 'mang their kind, hae freendships rife;

    Oor ranks they've thinned, aft quenched the life :

        Wi' shame be't tauld—

    Tae save their hooks, they've used the knife

        On young and auld :

" Tho' grey-haired sires, o' weakened arm,

    Their lure is fraught wi' deidly harm,

    Tae which they lend seductive charm,

        By sleight o' hand :

    I coonsel you, in accents warm,

        Tae shun their wand.

" Aft Tweedie ' breasts the lippin tide,'

    Tae seek ' the saumon in its pride : '

    If frae his lure ye a' flee wide,

        He'll yirm and fret,

    Or, thunderin', cleave the welkin wide

        Wi' ' Scotland Yet.'

" Heft him tae Tweed, tae kill his Kelt,

    Whare sic like feats o' him are telt,

Whare harried haunts hae aften felt
 His prowling greed;
And Keepers yearned his chafts tae welt:
 O' him tak heed.

" Thro' life he's been a rievin' thief—
 'Mang daurin' poachers aye the chief;
His reckless raids wrought fellest grief
 Whare'er he's been;
Mair lawless, schemin', heartless squief
 Was never seen.

" Jeff claims a loch he ca's his ain—
 A dirty dub, o'er which, aft fain
His lingle plies wi' micht and main
 Wi' birse and tether:
Send him toom hame, his strength tae hain,
 Tae stitch his leather.

" Bland Dr. Deft, deep versed in science,
 His weel flung flee aft tempts compliance;
Reject his drugs wi' firm defiance—
 Avoid his lance:
If skill 'gainst skill is your reliance,
 Ye've slender chance.

"TWEEDIE."

See page 43.

"JEFF."

See page 43.

" He sings o' 'trooties i' the burn,'
Gloats o'er their ' jinkin'' roun' ilk turn;
Hyne him far west, near auld Kilchurn,
    Tae fish Loch Awe;
Let ilk ane here exclaim in scorn,
    'Awa! Awa!'

" His glitt'rin' lure's a dang'rous dose ;
Ne'er let it dangle near ye'r nose,
Or soon ye may turn up ye'r toes,
    And bid farewcel ;
The doctor, he will you compose
    Within his creel.

" Cairnie, the mild, sedate, and douce,
Seems void o' pluck tae kill a louse ;
Wad shrink before a tim'rous mouse ;
    O' him beware :
When 'mang oor kind, he seems let loose
    Tae kill and snare.

" At scaling time he'll aye appear—
Nae need tae linger on the pier;
    D

His weel filled creel starts mony a tear

In drift and bay:

This meek-eed saint let nane draw near

Throughoot this day.

" That orator frae watery toon,

Wha spoots o' temp'rance nicht and noon,

O'er ' ribbon blue ' doth maudlin croon,

An emblem bricht!

A guide! a beacon! tae ilk loon

A shinin' licht :

" Though noo, through age, o' slackened zeal,

Was ance weel-kenned in drift and weil ;

Come! flout his lure, and mock his skeel—

An easy task;

Send him ashore, wi' nocht in creel

But emptied flask.

" Jason's a man o' means and skill ;

Failin' a fish he'll snatch its gill:

In roughish style he seeks tae kill,

E'en papers read,

Explainin' hoo oor bluid tae spill—

O' him tak heed :

" DR. DEFT."

See page 44.

"CAIRNIE."

See page 49.

" Send him adrift tae fish elsewhere;

Avoid his watchfu' glowerin' glare;

By throat, or fin, he may ensnare;

On him turn tail—

Tae Hieland haunts let him repair

Aroond Cuilfail.

" Young Athol Blair, keen-eyed, expert,

Will eager strive, intent, alert,

Firm in ye'r snoots tae fix his dart

If ye draw near—

Send him hum-drum, wi' dooncast heart,

Alang the pier.

" On him aye keep ye'r weather eye,

And o' his subtle float fecht shy;

Reject his phantom, shun his fly,

Thus save ye'r skin;

Send him toom hame, wi' basket dry,

Withoot a fin.

" MacTavish is a clansman rare ;

Baith fish and fowl he kens their lair;

He'll fearless face the snellest air
    Withoot a dram :
His raids are wide, he'll search wi' care
    Baith field and dam.

"Come! flaunt defiance in his face ;
  He's o' a cruel reckless race;
  Tae dee through him wad be disgrace
    Tae a' oor kind;
  'Mang ither frauds gie him nae place—
    Bear this in mind.

" Atlanta wields a deidly rod ;
  And, though his business lies abroad,
  He'll plund'rin' search through oor abode
    Wi' line and anchor;
  Oor hamesteads he doth aften load
    Wi' grief and rancour.

" This cruiser's keen, o' fell design ;
  When balmy warmth and breeze combine,
  Fu' mony a troot its life may tine—
    Be dragged tae earth,
  Unless they tae his weel-plied line
    Gie a wide ' berth.'

" THAT ORATOR FRAE WATERY TOON."

See page 50.

" JASON."

See page 50.

—

" Millman taps a' wi' wrigglin' worm ;

Though here denied his fav'rite charm,

Deem him not less a man o' harm,

  Where'er there's fish ;

He'll kill, and crood wi' deidly arm

  An ample dish.

" Beyond his taipe keep free o' scaith ;

Tae measure you he'll no be laith;

I charge ye a', wi' earnest braith,

  Tak utmost heed,

Lest, while he croonin' cuts his claith,

  We mourn oor deid.

" Fernie turns pale 'neath stiffened blast ;

Gie him a saft breeze frae the wast,

He'll deftly ply his killin' cast,

  And croosly craw ;

Tak tent o' him frae first tae last,

  And starve his maw.

" Ricardo wi' his wusps o' straw,

Wi' greedy leer and graspin' paw ;

His silk-worm 'raipe' withoot a flaw,
O' slend'rest girth,
Yet strong eneuch for you tae draw
Tae upper earth.

" Frae Glen. the mute. a' widely steer :
O' varnished rods and lines keep clear;
Wi' you as spoil he'll no be sweer
Tae burst his bag;
Send him back ',clean' tae his veneer:
Silence his brag.

" Horatio is a man o' blude,
Draws victims rowth frae field and flude;'
Like Bluebeard, as 'tis understood
He wields the steel;
Send him ashore in silent mood :
Wi' empty creel.

" Roy Baulderston, o' vast pretence,
A man o' bounce, and void o' mense,
Wi' ardour keen, o' subtle sense:
Flee yont his reach;
'Twixt him and you keep a wide fence—
The greedy leech.

"YOUNG ATHOLE BLAIR."

See page 55

"MACTAVISH."

See page 55.

E

" There's ither weeds, 'twere lang tae name,
     Weel kenned in mony a harried hame—
     Oor blude they've shed tae fill their wame,
          And dainty dine;
     The greedy whelps! as void o' shame
          As snortin' swine.

" This Club, 'neath name o' guileless Saint,
     Affects tae be withoot a taint;
     And yet its deeds, what words can paint;
          Brimfu' o' guile:
     They mak me reel, ma heart turn faint ;
          Sae black, sae vile.

" Think o' the host o' kindred killed,
     The anguish coontless hearts has thrilled—
     The best blude o' oor Loch's been spilled
          By miscreants mean;
     Oh ! wad some creature, vulture-billed,
          Snatch oot their een.

" When o'er the lost I inward pore,
     Think o' the loved I'll meet no more,

Wi' longings deep, smote tae the core,

Ma heart is torn;

O'er cherished freends, reft frae life's shore,

I pine and mourn.

" Nae mair 'neath autumn's gowden gleam

They'll buoyant cleave their native stream,

Nae mair wi' amorous ardour beam

In wedlock blist;

Their memory's noo a fadin' dream,

Like mornin' mist.

" When doon the postern o' the past

My askin' ee I pensive cast;

Reca' the hoors owre bricht tae last,

Hoo deep ma gloom!

Sae mony mates hae 'neath life's blast

Met early doom!

" Few, few are here tae tell the tale,

Recoont the hopes that swelled life's sail.

Sped oor bricht coorse 'neath fav'rin' gale,

Through radiant hoors

O'er mates lang lost we pine and wail,

Nae langer oors.

"ATLANTA."

See page 56.

" MILLMAN."

See page 61.

" Oor ranks arc thinned, life's dull and lanc—

 Oor best and dearest noo arc ganc ;

 Auld echoes o' the past noo manc

  In minor key,

Sae sad, sae sweet, though left alanc—

  Their tones soothe me.

" We ken the past : nanc can forsee

 The ills we'll meet, the doom we'll dree,

 Or 'ncath what fate we'll close oor ee ;

  May kinsmen here,

Hooever fu' o' sport or glee,

  Tae me gic ear :

" On a' within oor envied mere

 I'd fain enjoin, a prudent fear

 O' men in boats wi' fishin' gear ;

  Their presence spurn ;

Flee yont their reach when they appear—

  Flee yont return.

" Spring may anew redeck the plain,

 Oor peerless lilies bloom again,

But wha ma loved mates o' the main
Can e'er restore?
O'er me, corrodin' grief maun reign,
For evermore.

" Kindred and freends, the hoor draws near—
The Club will sally frae the pier,
Tae search ilk sweep wi' greedy leer,
Tae catch and kill;
Speed forth! proclaim through bank and weir
Ma royal will:

" Reject and shun a' floatin' food,
Hooever thick the flees may crood;
The wolves are here in hungry mood
Tae tak oor lives;
Ilk ane wha shuns this rav'nous brood
He langest thrives.

" There's plenty larvæ in the deep,
The luscious snails in thoosands creep;
The maggot, fund on shelvin' steep;
Is zestfu' fare;
Ne'er turn ye'r heid tae tak a peep
Tae upper air:

"RICARDO."

See page 61.

"GLEN."

See page 62.

" Speed forth throughoot oor utmost boond,

   Fleet as the hart before the hoond;

   Enjoin on kinsmen a' aroond,

       In earnest mood,

   This day, to shun, through drift and soond,

       A' surface food.

" I'll wait the issue o' the day;

   Let nane ma mandate disobey,

   Lest thae fell skunks should on you prey,

       And lap ye'r blude,

   And drape oor haunts in black array,

       Throughoot the flude."

Swift as the swallow on the wing

The scouts sped forth in circling ring :

In eager haste, they clove their way

Through drift and deep, through bank and bay ;

From "Scart" to pier, from "Manse" to "Sluice,"

To warn of Mungo's crew let loose—

Through every haunt, around each isle,

To ply their lure with artful wile.

The warning bruited through each sound,
Deep boding fears o'erspread each bound;
Prompt councils met in deep and bay,
Framed wise precautions 'gainst the day,
Expressed their hearts in grateful phrase,
Nor failed their thoughtful Sire to praise.

In jocund mood the Club drew near;
The boatmen busied on the pier;
The glistening rods in morning sun,
The glee, the banter, and the fun;
Kind greetings thrown from boat to boat,
Ere yet they from the pier had shot;
Sights such as these, too seldom seen,
So bright, so brief; too rare, I ween—
Fain would I linger o'er this scene.

The air was warm, and hopes swelled high,
Bright gleaming in each eager eye;
The gilding sun 'mong clouds arrayed,
Lent to the Loch a softened shade;
Mild eastern breezes gently blew,
Slight ripples o'er the waters threw;

"HORATIO."

See page 62.

F

" In jocund mood the Club drew near,
The boatmen busied on the pier."

See page 80.

Light fleecy clouds of sober grey—
Auspicious promise for the day—
Hung high o'erhead, o'erspread the lift,
Lent to each bay, each bank and drift,
That sheen so dear to angler's eyes—
A sheen which only anglers prize.

While boatmen busied with their craft,
Securely fixing fore and aft,
Ere laggard time had played her part
To crown desire, ring out a start,
Uranus, leader of his band,
Who, tip-toe, longed to quit the strand,
To seize their rods and breast the main,
Flung to his mates this stirring strain :—

The Leader's Song.

(AIR—"*When the Kye come hame.*")

" Pull up, my lads, make ready—
    Nor choose a better day ;
All boats wi' anchor steady ;
    I'm itching for the fray.

The breeze is blawing saftly,
The sun is in the shade ;
Each rod and reel rig deftly,
Make ready for our raid.

Make ready for our raid, boys,
Make ready for our raid ;
Each rod and reel rig deftly,
Make ready for our raid.

" To-day, we scorn life's bustle,
Frae din and drive we're free ;
Each eager for the tussle,
Hope glints in every ee.
The flies dance on the billow,
The fish are on the feed ;
Let each man grasp his willow—
Come ! wish each other speed.

Come ! wish each other speed, boys, &c.

" I'm panting for the rally :
Come ! man your boats, nor stay ;
Let's to the contest sally,
Nor hame till close o' day.

" Oh ! what else so enchanting ?

   Oh ! wha can name a sport ?

Let dullards deem it vaunting—

   The langest day's too short.

     The langest day's too short, boys, &c.

" Then to your boats, and lithely

   Fish teeming drift and weil ;

At nicht let each come blithely

   And show a well-filled creel.

I spurn puir victims' mangling

   On upland, muir, or lea—

The wale o' sport is angling,

   A fishing day for me.

     A fishing day for me, boys,

      A fishing day for me—

     The wale o' sport is angling,

      A fishing day for me."

The signal given, each oar was grasped,

Straight from the shore the boatmen dashed,

With lusty arm, and eager heart,

With inward aim to play their part.

Each craft steered straight for chosen point,

Each line examined, scanned each joint,

Each heart quick panting for the fray;

It was the wished—the longed for day

For test of skill through bank and bay.

The fleet-winged gull is on the feed,

Skimming the Loch with dipping speed,

Assurance this of flies afloat,

Which cheers the inmates of each boat;

The swallow, twittering in mid air,

Regales itself on light-winged fare;

The lonely heron flapping soars,

Its scream is heard 'long willowed shores;

The graceful swan with archéd wings,

A wide extending ripple flings;

The wild duck, with her callow train,

From reedy banks now seeks the main;

Her deep maternal yearnings warm,

To shield her brood from hurt and harm,

Have oft me stirred, my thoughts oft raised

To Him, who is too little praised—

He, who presides and rules o'er all,

Who even notes the sparrow's fall;

Who decks the lily, clothes the plain,

Keeps watch and ward o'er land and main;

How oft I've felt, when blessings crowned,

The loving Giver was not owned.

As merry youngsters, in their prime,

Pant for the fun of festal time;

As pent-up boys, let loose from school,

Will sally forth, hearts free and full;

Or ardent lads, and maidens gay,

Rush forth to spend blithe holiday

On sunny banks, in bosky bowers—

How brief, how fleet, such wingéd hours.

So votaries of the gentle art

Oft leave their care to play their part;

Recall the hours, re-live the past,

Of happy days too bright to last.

Saint Mungo's Club oft courts the tide,

And who will dare their choice to chide?

Far from the city's din and strife

To woo and win its glancing life;

But rapture felt, each sudden joy,
Is ever blent with some alloy—
Like golden dreams that fade away,
How fast doth flit the longest day!

But to our tale: each point was gained,
Each drift they sought was now attained;
Each plied his lure with artful wile,
The longed-for beauties to beguile.
Long while they fished, without avail,
Boat sent to boat complaining wail:
Hours passed away, and still no sign:
No life was felt, no throbbing line;
Far as the clearest eye could reach,
No movement seen from beach to beach—
No circling ripple, plopping sound,
Was seen or heard, through all around;
So loath, so sullen, slow to rise,
No trout yet met their longing eyes.

Deep disappointment wrung each heart;
For lack of skill, no one need smart.
Had they not oft in other days,
Along these drifts, and through these bays,

Filled high their panniers deep and wide,

And borne them to the pier with pride?

And yet to-day they seemed accurst;

'Mong luckless days this was the worst—

Not one faint bite, not one slight rise,

However deftly plied their flies,

Did reach their hand, or greet their eyes.

'Twas wonderful! mysterious! strange!

From " Mary's Isle " to " Duncan's Range,"

Thro' " Horse Shoe " pot to " Beech Hedge " end

Full many a well-manned boat did wend ;

Along the " Shallows," through each deep,

In eager quest keen anglers sweep :

The Club had fished each drift and bay,

And that, throughout most faultless day—

And yet, alas! 'twas bootless play!

Time fled apace, the day wore on,

Tired anglers now were heard to moan;

From boat to boat blank tidings went,

With clam'rous plaints the air was rent.

Late in the day boats gathering thronged ;

Fierce imprecations, loud, prolonged,

Wide o'er the barren waters flew,
From beaten boatmen, baffled crew.

One boatman swore, "It's devilish strange:
Is there nae sign o' coming change?
I've fished this loch time oot o' mind—
In calm, in sunshine, rain, and wind;
But this infernal day caps a'
The auldest 'mang us ever saw.
We've seen fish dour, aft bitin' shy,
Refuse baith minnow, phantom, fly;
I'm fear'd there's mair than usual wrang:
Tae see sae mony toom boats thrang
That's raiked and plewed baith beech and bay,
Yet deil a fish we've seen the day.
Some twenty rods frae morn till now,
A' eident plied frae stern and bow;
It beggars a', dumfoun'ers me,
Tae ken what's wrang I canna see!
Auld Nick, wi' a' his imps o' hell,
Couldna hae wrought mair deevlish spell!
A Club o' men, o' weel kent skeel,
Tae fish ilk deep, ilk drift, and weil,

Without one scale to croon their keel!
It's past belief!   Some damning cause
Quhilk far transcends auld Nature's laws
Must be at wark.   'Tis yevident,
Some spitefu' fiend o' vile intent,
Tae mar oor sport seems keenly bent.
Why troots this day refused oor flees
Is mair than I can analeese!
Rax me ma pipe; I'll hae a blast—
Nae yerthly use tae cast and cast;
Tak ma advice, strike for the shore,
Ye'll tell a tale ne'er tauld before."

Uranus, captain of the host,
Addressed his mates, " clean " from each coast ;
Expressed bewilderment, surprise,
Refused to name, or e'en surmise,
The cause of this day's dire defeat,
So galling, puzzling, so complete ;
Transcending ought he ever heard,
Like, awesome tale of mystic bard :
Result so gruesome, strange, and weird,
Would ever by this Club be feared.

The day's conditions all combined

To charge with hope each angler's mind—

The light, the breeze, the freshened wave ;

The swarming flies high promise gave

Of splendid sport, of gleesome play,

Thro' teeming drift and bounteous bay ;

And yet, all here, each boat a blank !

As if they'd fished some poisoned tank ;

Made victims of some hellish prank !

Such strange enchantment, sorcerer's spell,

Such witchery no tongue could tell !

Like " favourite," nowhere in the field,

All former honours now must yield ;

Like laurelled wrestler prostrate flung,

Whose past achievements oft had wrung,

Loud plaudits from his rude compeers—

His victor now, draws forth their cheers ;

Like gallant soldier tired and worn,

The colours leaves, he oft had borne—

And glory won, nor sought retreat ;

But beaten now, must own defeat :

So baffled anglers grieve and moan,

"Uranus, pointing, raised his head,
And to his downcast comrades said,—

See Page 97.

Rehearse old feats long past and gone,

Recount the "takes" of other days,

When crowded creels, and well-won bays,

Earned for their Club an envied name ;

How now, alas ! How fled that fame ?

Uranus, pointing, raised his head,

And to his downcast comrades said—

" Let's strike for home: in order, range ;

We've tried the phantom, found no change :

With measured oar let's slowly steer,

To own with shame upon the pier

Our dire defeat, each baffled scheme,

Surpassing aught e'er dreamed in dream."

From stricken hearts, subdued and sad,

Which morning found so buoyant, glad,

Low mutterings now, more deep than loud,

Were uttered by the awestruck crowd ;

As, slowly through the waves they pushed,

An eerie dread, the boldest hushed,

Lest oozy wraith should upward creep,

To clutch and whelm them in the deep.

With furtive glance, and trembling oar,

They gravely trawled the "kirk-yard" shore ;

With haunted hearts, and aspect drear,

In pensive mood each crew drew near,

And moored its boat, longside the pier :

One lank, lean pike, three dappled perch—

The joint result of long day's search,

'Mid vengeful curses, fierce and low—

Were all St. Mungo's men could show.

This Club of skillful, staunch, good men,

Afraid of naught in human ken ;

Of dauntless hearts, as daring, brave,

As ever rode a crested wave,

And yet, to-day, some occult spell

Arose their courage bold to quell :

A preternatural fear and dread

Alarmed each heart, amazed each head.

How oft 'tis thus ! Freed from alarm,

We prompt aver we feared no harm ;

When no real dangers us confront

We'll steadfast stand; bear any brunt :

In absence of menacing foe

We promptly render blow for blow.

" One lank, lean pike, three dappled perch,
The joint result of long day's search."

See page 98.

So with this Club; safe on the strand,

With angry accents, brandished wand,

Now freed from wraith, from creatures dire,

Anglers and boatmen vent their ire;

Loud grew their clamour, coarse and strong,

Protesting 'gainst some unknown wrong ;

Their frantic bellowing, mad despair,

In deafening accents rent the air;

Ne'er was such vaunting, baffled pride,

Thrown, thwart and far, o'er Leven's tide :

'Bove this loud strife, this frenzied blood,

An eldricht scream rung from the flood :

A Kelpie grey, with slimy front,

Of loathsome mein, clung to a punt,

And, mocking sat, with jeering tongue,

Clear to the shore, this utterance flung :

Kelpie's Caution.

" What ? men in tears! come, cease your blare!

Will fretting fetch you better fare?

To learn the cause o' your despair,

List to the words o' Kelpic :

" Your murmuring grunts throughout this day,

    E'en ane o' my cauld blude made wae,

    To note, when baffled in the fray,

        Hoo sairly it did skelp ye.

" I want ere yet you leave this strand,

    While each takes doon his bludeless wand,

    To let ilk man clear understand

        That I am here to help ye.

" Like you, I'm come o' ancient blude ;

    Tho' maist a native o' the flude,

    Queer pranks I've played through wild and wood—

        I'm deemed a dangerous whelpie.

" Yestreen, a monarch o' the deep,

    Unseen beneath the pier did creep,

    Heard plots aloft which made him weep ;

        He warned his kind to welt ye :

" When Commodores instruct their crew,

    Aye shun the pier, keep oot o' view ;

    Lest like disaster should ensue,

        Keep close within your sheltie.

" A Kelpie grey, with slimy front,
Of loathsome mein, clung to a punt."

See page 101.

" Each haunt oot ower the Loch this nicht

Will glow wi' phosphorescent licht,

When all will meet in banquet bricht,

      Frae sire to leanest Keltic.

In circling shoals they'll gaily sing,

Wi' mirth they'll mak their floodgates ring,

Loud mocking taunts will freely fling

      Until they cleave the welkie.

" When next by ' Mary's Castle ' grey

To ' Gairney Mouth ' you cleave your way,

Or seek ' Green Isle ' in northern bay,

      Mak freends wi' tricky Kelpie :

" For Kelpie he's a gruesome blade,

      Clever Kelpie, cunning Kelpie ;

Like you, he's in the killing trade,   .

      Just leave your creels to Kelpie."

He ceased ; he scanned the awe-struck crew—

His wrinkled form rose full on view ;

Distended, huge, his filmy eyes,

11

The boldest filled with mute surprise :
This oozy spectre, tall and grim,
His hideous shape, each webbed limb
Poised on the punt, glanced 'long the pier,
Sent snorting laugh, sardonic leer,
Then lithely flapped his massive tail,
When waves uprose, as if a gale
Had smote the Loch with tempest weird—
When Kelpie sank, and disappeared.

At first sight of this Gorgon vast,
St. Mungo's veterans stood aghast ;
With quaking hearts, and curdling blood
They eyed this monster of the flood,
Transfixed with fear, charged with affright ;
More hideous form ne'er met their sight;
With breathless awe and deep alarm
They learned the cause of all their harm;
Their bitter blank throughout the day
To heightened wonder now gave way :
Subdued and mute they leave the pier,
No one finds words his mate to cheer;
Their thoughts so wrapt, their hearts so drear.

Unlike the feats of arms of old

In tournaments, by Minstrels told,

When in the dust a knight was flung,

While plaudits free from courtiers rung,

The victor proudly claimed the glove

As trophy for his lady-love :

No victor here! no honours won!

Like unhorsed knight, all vanquished, done!

Abashed and galled they slow retire,

Each muttering moans of fret and ire ;

Each aching heart with anguish torn,

Tired and morose they homeward turn ;

Each weary wight, collapsed and worn :

Dejected, hopeless, sad, forlorn.

No vintage left, to lighten care ;

No cheering draught to soothe despair—

Oh! name it not, each creel and pocket

Had naught but flask drained to its socket!

It was not thus in other days,

When song and banter oft they'd raise,

While victors proudly claimed their bays.

The Captain lists Uranus' tale,
Endorsed by many a moaning wail ;
'Wildered he stands, aghast to hear—
No tale so weird e'er met his ear.

To Harry's home they fain repair,
The bounties of his board to share;
With thoughtful haste he meets each want,
From *menu* neither scrimp nor scant,
Doles forth to each in freest style ;
And seeks, by kindness, to beguile,
To sooth all, 'neath their dire defeat,
While yet within his snug retreat.

Regaled with daintiest fare, they leave,
Still prone o'er their mishaps to grieve ;
They sought the train and westward flew:
More baffled men, more joyless crew,
From loved Lochleven ne'er withdrew.